TRASH & CAN-IT

WRITER: WAŊBDI' ŠDA
ART: ANTHONY TAN
COLORS: YUMUL R ROHVEL
COVER: ANTHONY TAN & YUMUL R. ROHVEL
ADDITIONAL ART: ZAC ATKINSON & JOSE CARLOS SILVA
LETTERS: WILSON RAMOS

EDITOR-IN-CHIEF: JOSHUA WERNER
ART DIRECTOR: MARTHA WEBBY
WWW.SOURCEPOINTKIDS.COM

CHAPTER ONE

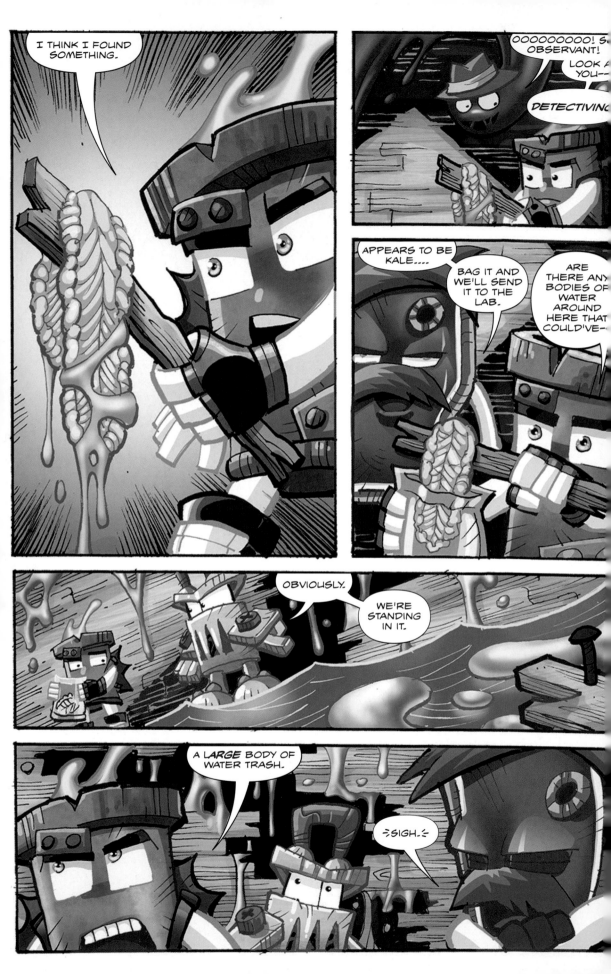

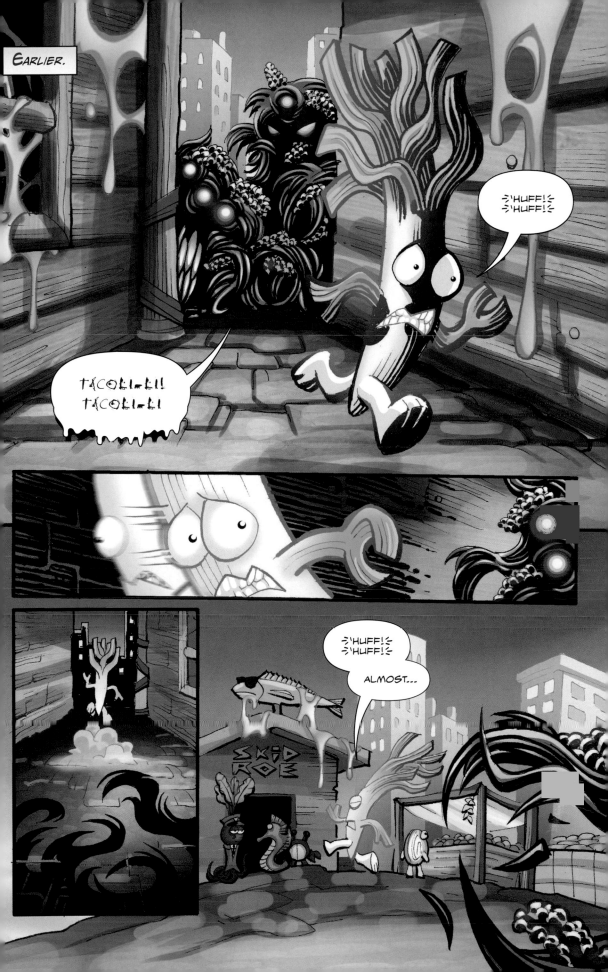

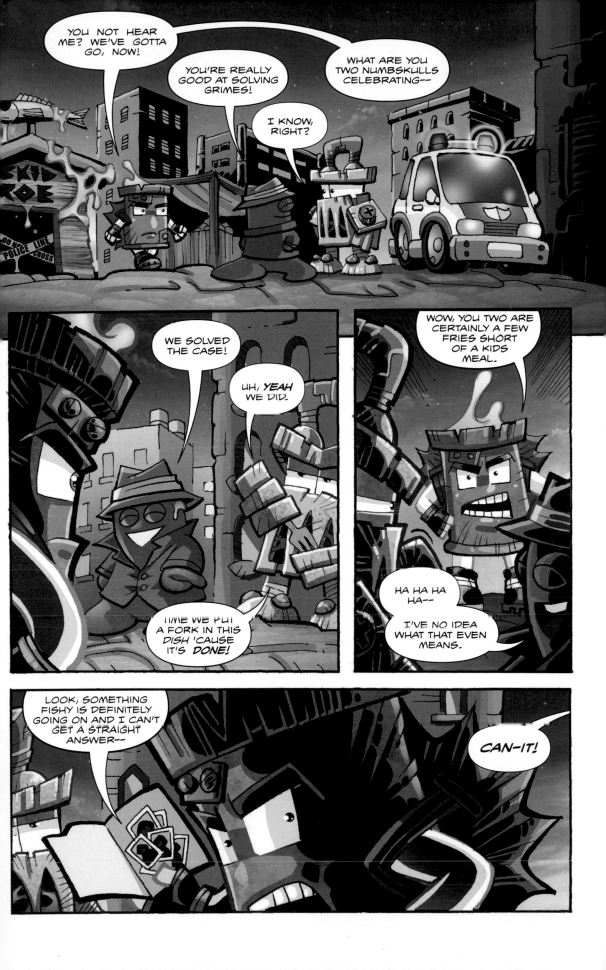

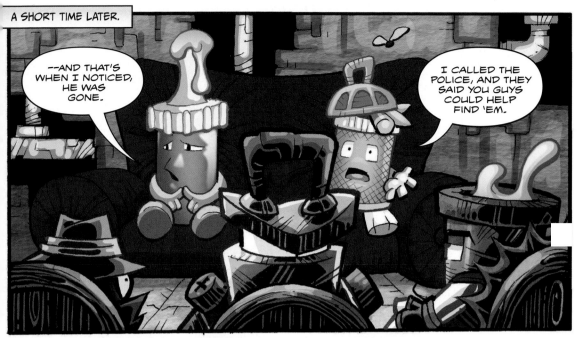

--AND THAT'S WHEN I NOTICED, HE WAS GONE.

I CALLED THE POLICE, AND THEY SAID YOU GUYS COULD HELP FIND 'EM.

YOUR STUFFY.

HIS NAME IS *BLUE.*

UH HUH. UH HUH.

AND HOW WOULD YOU DESCRIBE *BLUE.*

HE'S CUDDLY AND SNUGGLY! SUPER SOFT AND DIJON'S BESTEST BUDDY IN THE WHOLE--

YES, *BUT* WHAT COLOR WOULD YOU SAY *BLUE* IS?

BLUE?

GOT IT.

SO BLUE IS BLUE.

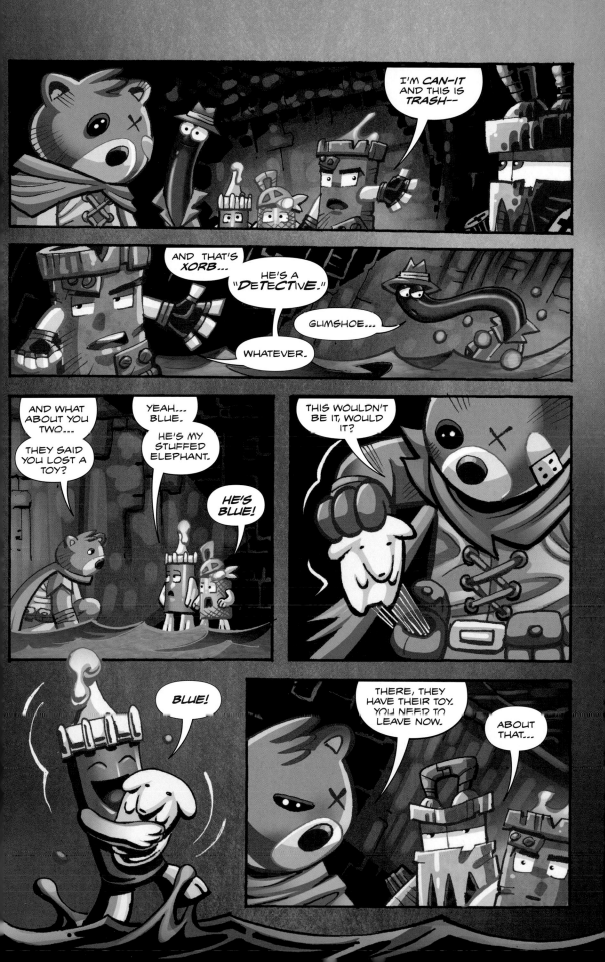

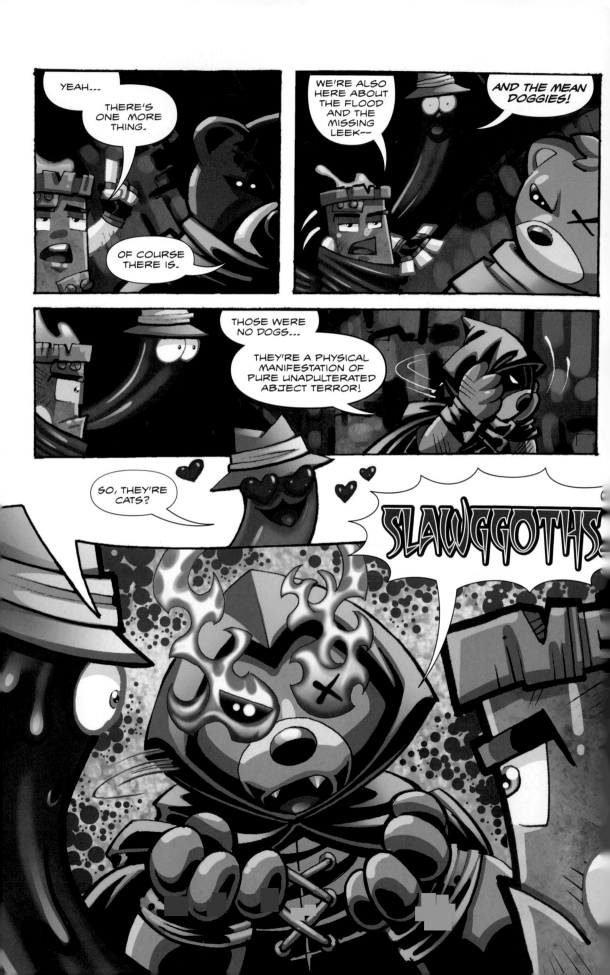

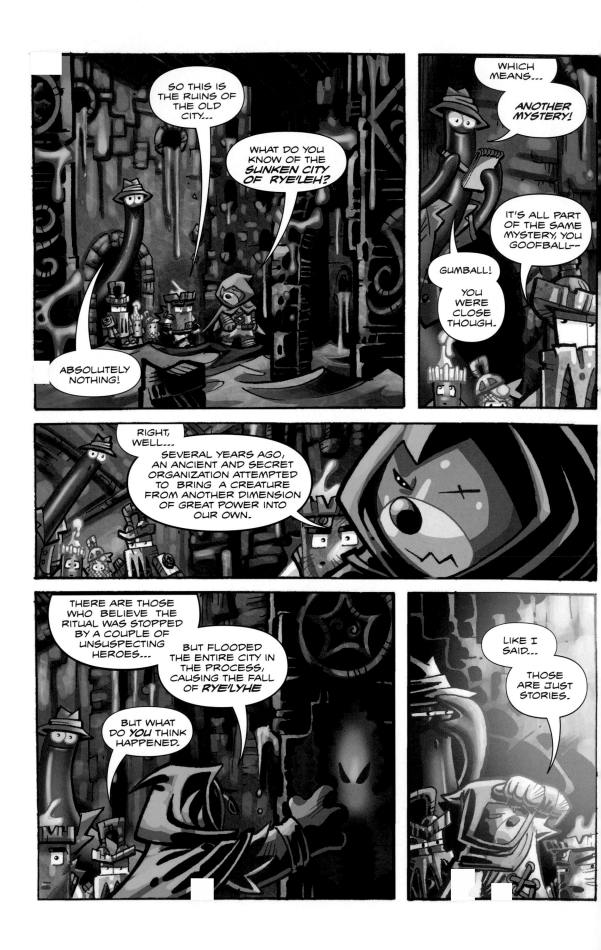

CHAPTER THREE

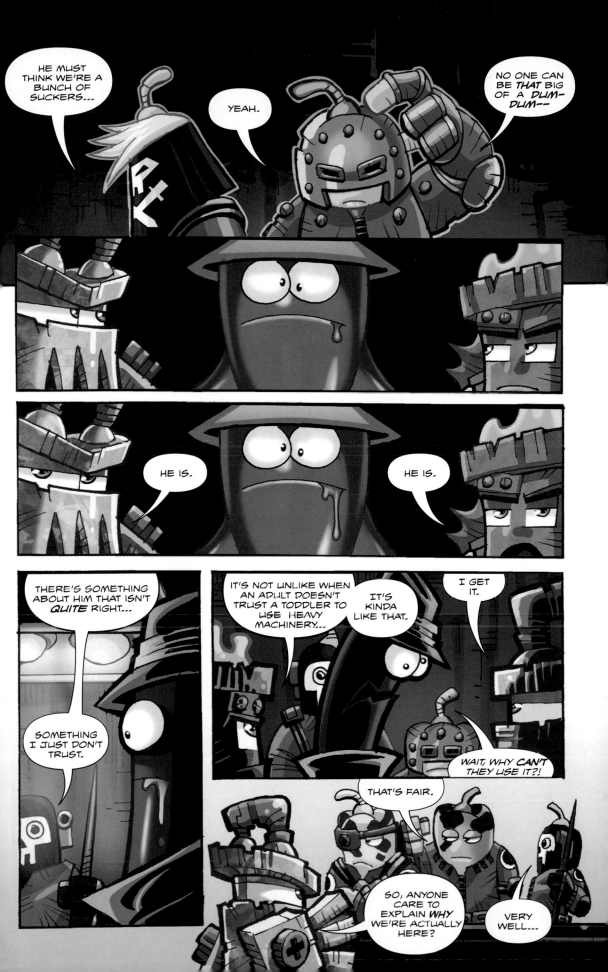

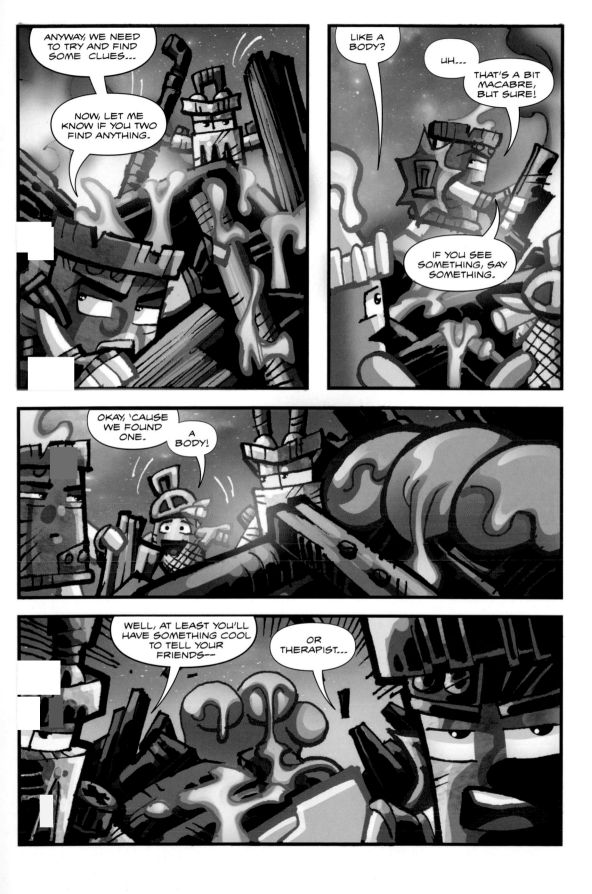

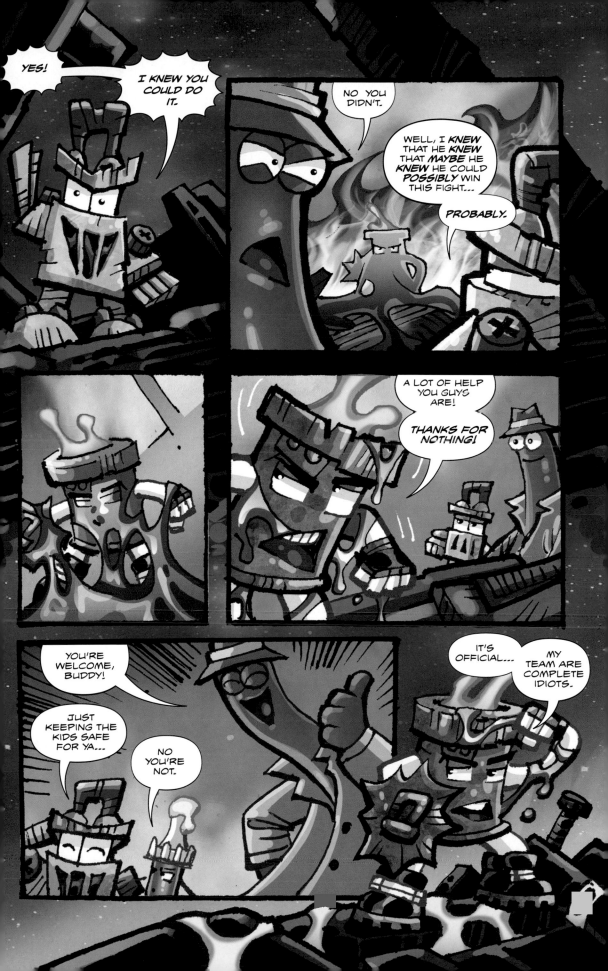

CHAPTER FOUR

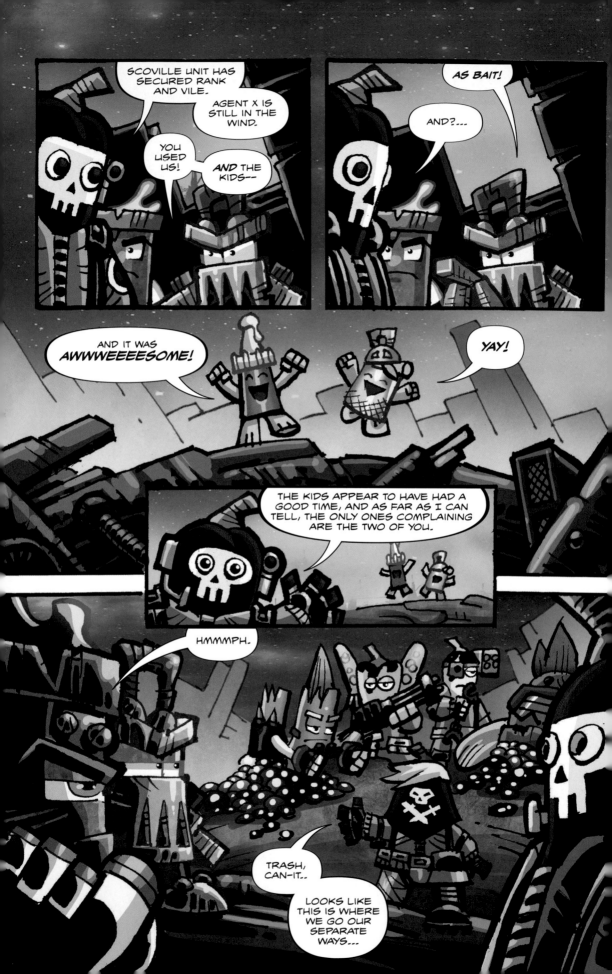

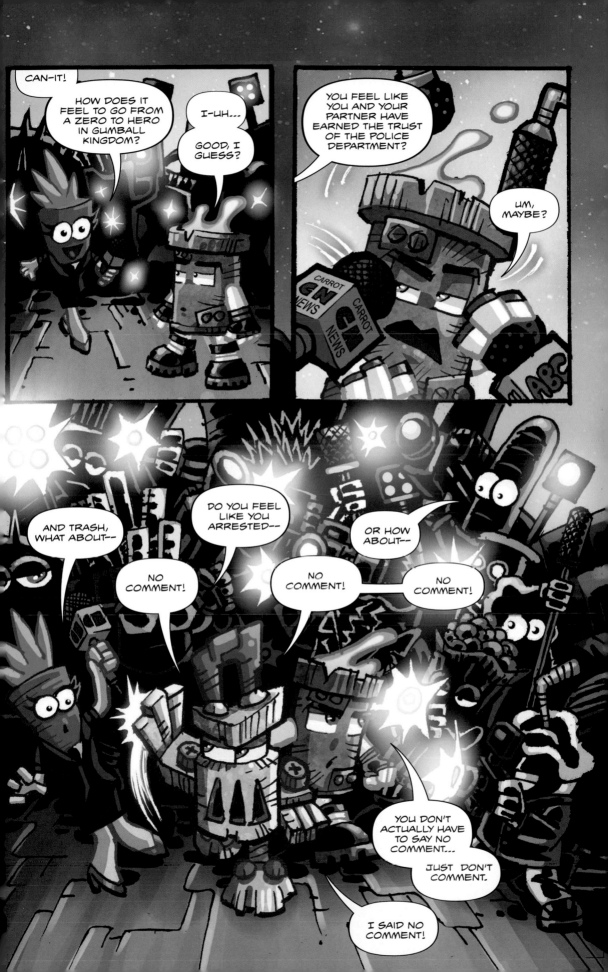

TRASH & CAN-IT

COVER GALLERY

ISSUE #1 COVER (JOSE CARLOS SILVA

ISSUE #2 COVER (ANTHONY TAN)

ISSUE #3 COVER (ANTHONY TAN

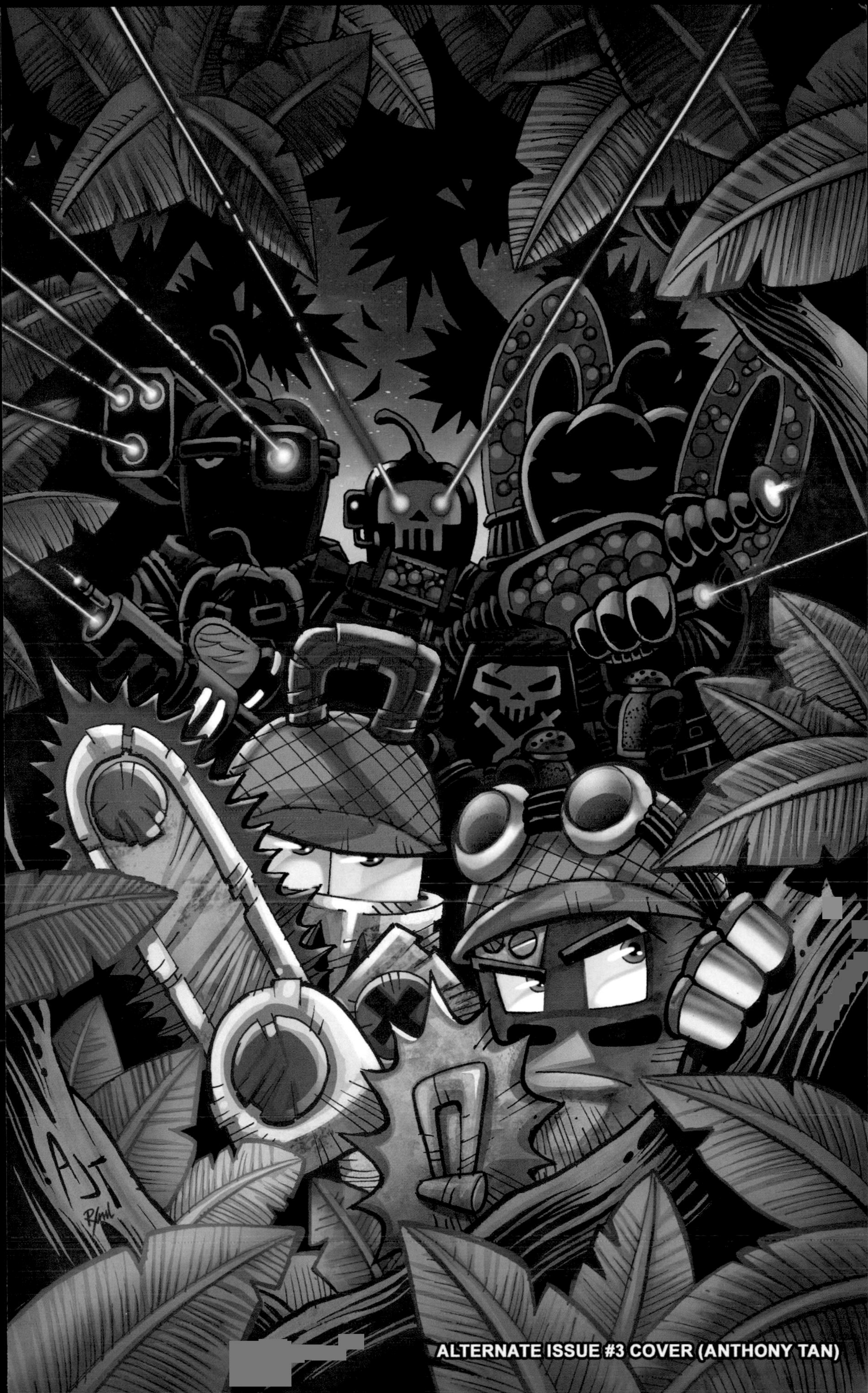

ALTERNATE ISSUE #3 COVER (ANTHONY TAN)

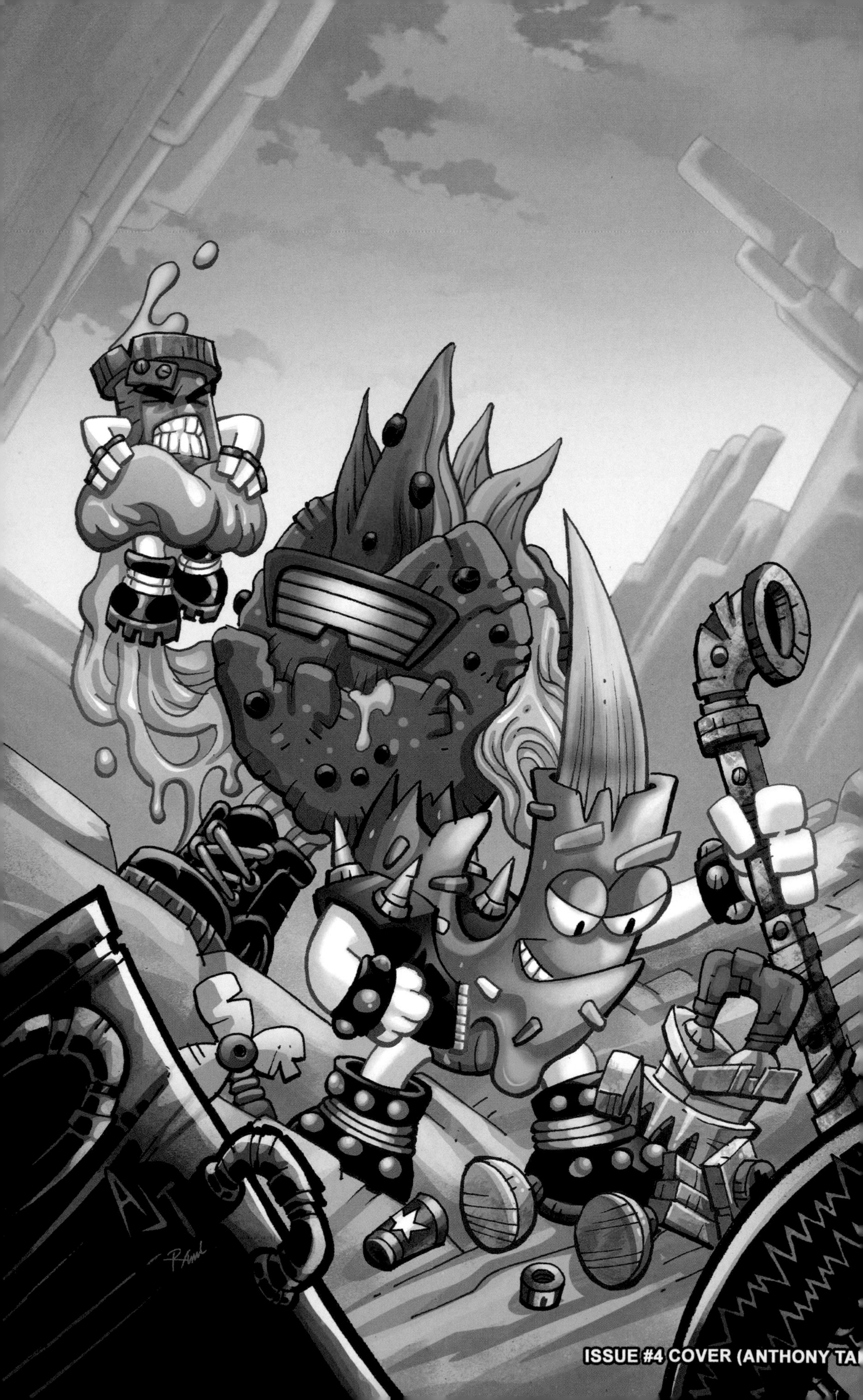

ISSUE #4 COVER (ANTHONY TA

ALTERNATE COVER (ZAC ATKINSON)

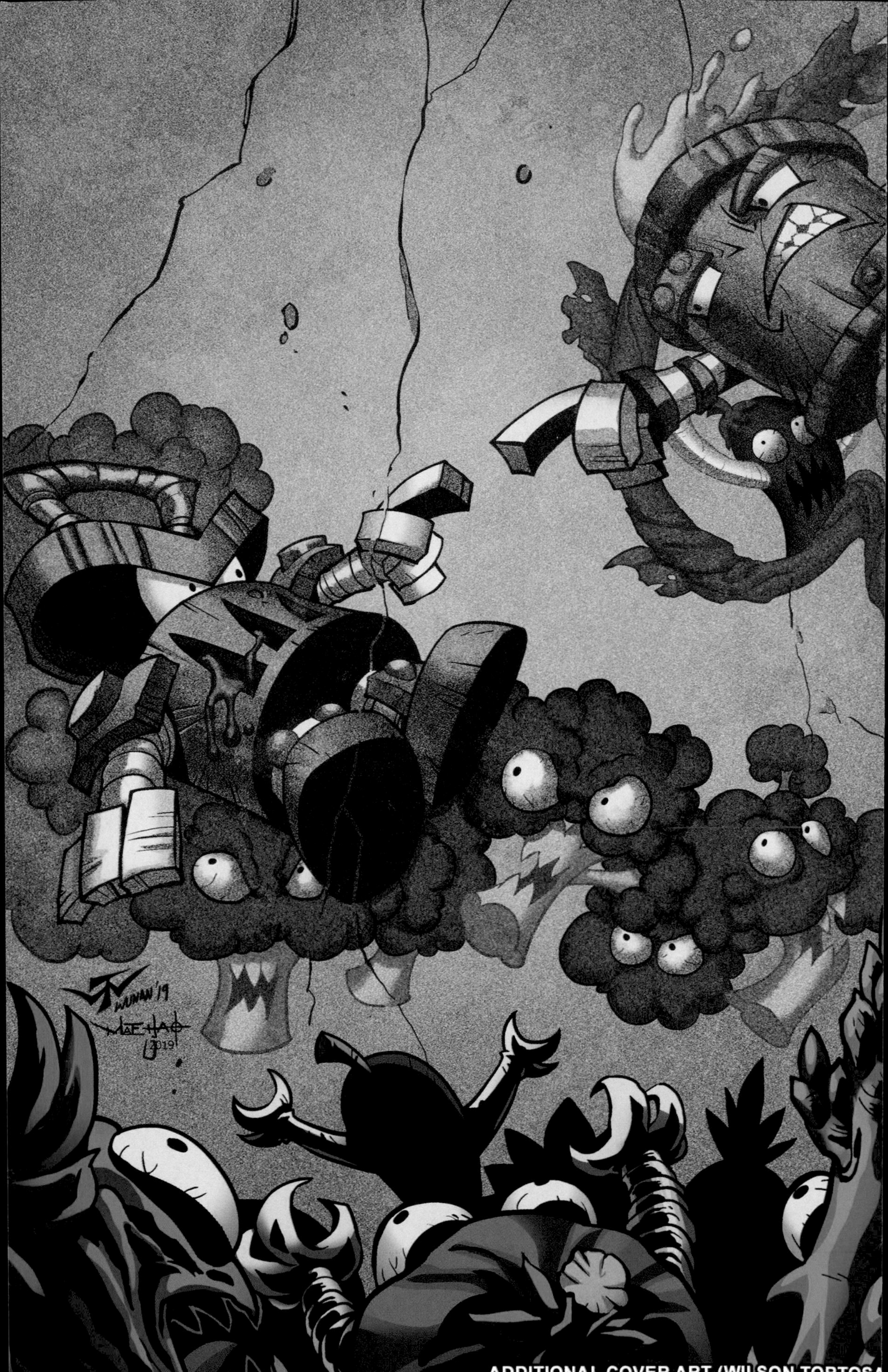

ADDITIONAL COVER ART (WILSON TORTOSA

EARLY CONCEPT ART: ANTHONY TAN

CAN-IT FIRST PASS

CAN-IT SECOND PASS

CAN-IT THIRD PASS

CAN-IT FINAL PASS

RASH CHARACTER DESIGN

XORB DESIGN

MAYOR MCGUMBALL

EVOLUTION OF LOGO DESIGNS